Siân's children's stories are about friendship, love and kindness that you want to read again and again. With beautiful illustrations and heartfelt characters, Siân aims to enchant and inspire readers to feel special about who they are.

Siân lives in Wales where she treasures the time spent with her friends and family. She works as a Human Resources Manager who stumbled into writing when the global pandemic hit.

Copyright © Siân Phillips 2023

The right of **Siân Phillips** to be identified as author of this work has been asserted by the author in accordance with sections 77 and 78 of the Copyright, Designs and Patents Act 1988.

All rights reserved. No part of this publication may be reproduced, stored in a retrieval system, or transmitted in any form or by any means, electronic, mechanical, photocopying, recording, or otherwise, without the prior permission of the publishers.

Any person who commits any unauthorised act in relation to this publication may be liable to criminal prosecution and civil claims for damages.

A CIP catalogue record for this title is available from the British Library.

ISBN 9781398458376 (Paperback)
ISBN 9781398458383 (ePub e-book)

www.austinmacauley.com

First Published 2023
Austin Macauley Publishers Ltd®
1 Canada Square
Canary Wharf
London
E14 5AA

This book is dedicated to my parents who have always encouraged and supported me in the journey that is life.

This is a story about a little boy called Tom, who is eight years old and his new friend Smokey, the dragon.

One warm sunny morning, Tom was helping his mum in the kitchen making a stew for lunch. Tom's mum asked him to wash up the dishes and the utensils they had used. Tom hated doing the dishes, but he loved to help his mum.

Standing by the sink that overlooked the greenhouse in the garden, Tom saw something move. He thought it might have been a mouse or even a hedgehog. When Tom finished the dishes, he went outside to explore.

He didn't find a mouse or a hedgehog, but hiding behind the old flower pots was...

A baby dragon, shivering because he was scared. Tom was a bit scared himself because he had read about dragons breathing fire. Tom sat and watched him for a while and then decided to pick him up very carefully and take him inside the house. Tom showed his mum what he had found. They placed the baby dragon in a box, and he fell asleep.

When the baby dragon woke up, Tom and his mother were eating their stew. They heard an almighty rumble; it was the baby dragons' tummy!

Tom asked his mum, 'What do dragons eat?'

She said, 'I don't know.' So, they decided to give the baby dragon a bowl of stew. The baby dragon loved it and ate it all up.

Over the next couple of days while they we deciding what to do with their new friend, Tom and his mum named the baby dragon Smokey, because he was not yet big enough to breathe fire!

Smokey had a big appetite and ate everything Tom's mum made for him. Tom's mum decided to make some welsh cakes. Smokey loved them! He gobbled them all up and forgot to leave any for other people.

Smokey struggled to sleep at night. Tom hated reading, but it's the only thing that helped Smokey sleep. Each night, Tom went to his book-shelf and picked out a magical story to read to Smokey until he fell asleep.

A week had gone by and still Tom and his mum had not decided what they must do with Smokey. They could not keep him as he was a dragon, and they can grow really big.

The next day, they took a trip to the supermarket to stock up on groceries. Tom was too young to stay at home by himself, and Smokey could not stay in the house by himself either. So Tom and his mum decided to take Smokey with them. They hid Smokey in Tom's rucksack. Smokey had never seen a supermarket before, so it was an adventure for him.

When they got home, Tom thought it would be good to go into the garden and play football and teach Smokey how to play. Unfortunately, it didn't last long. When Smokey bit the ball, it burst.

They went indoors to play a board game instead and chose to play snakes and ladders. It was fun and Tom now had a new friend to play with.

One evening while Tom was sleeping, he could hear a crying coming from the kitchen. He ran downstairs to find Smokey standing by the back door looking out. Tom opened the door and staring back at him were two red eyes. Tom started to shake with fright. After rubbing his eyes, he realised that it was Smokey's mum. She had come back to collect him!

Tom picked up Smokey and give him a hug before putting him on his mum's back. Tom wiped his eyes. He was going to miss his new friend, but he knew that Smokey had to be with his mum.

Smokey's mum flew off into the night sky. As she flew, she breathed fire into the night sky. It swirled and twirled into the words 'thank you'. Tom saw them and smiled.

Ingram Content Group UK Ltd.
Milton Keynes UK
UKHW020921110623
423187UK00008B/142